Gunn

D0513469

Two in One

THE LOST GIANT

and

BIGGER, BIGGEST, BEST

ILLUSTRATED BY CLAIRE MUMFORD

P

PARRAGON

This is a Parragon Book

©Parragon 1997

Parragon
13-17 Avonbridge Trading Estate
Atlantic Road, Avonmouth
Bristol. BS11 9QD

Produced by The Templar Company plc,
Pippbrook Mill, London Road, Dorking,
Surrey RH4 1JE

All rights reserved

Designed by Janie Louise Hunt
Edited by Caroline Steeden
Printed and bound in Italy
ISBN 0 75252 500 X

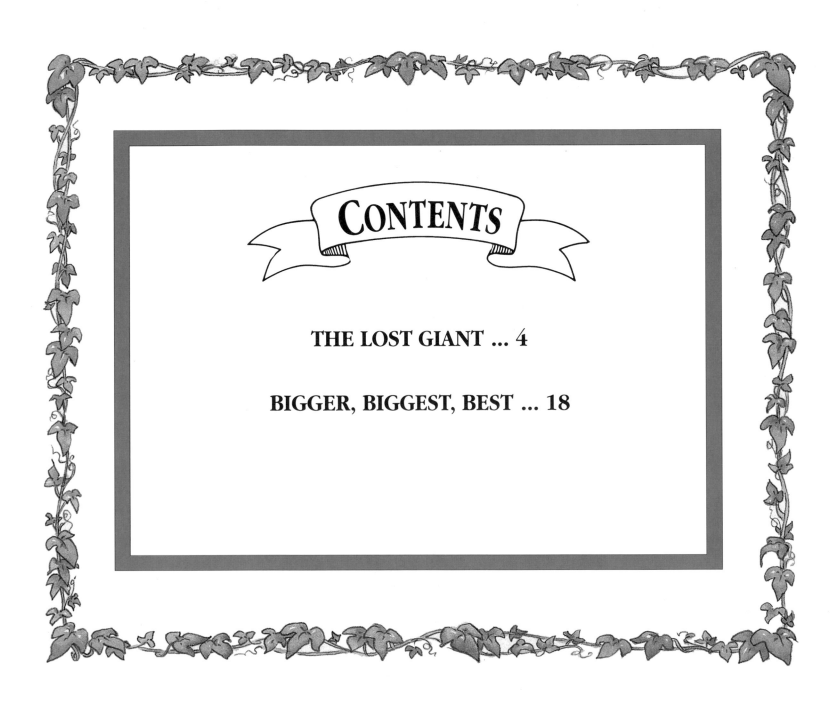

CONTENTS

THE LOST GIANT

WRITTEN BY AMBER HUNT

The air wobbled a bit, shimmered, swirled and with a 'whoomph' a rather bewildered, twelve-foot giant appeared. He was only a very young giant, and looked rather like any other young boy — except he was slightly larger, of course!

"Oh dear," said the giant, stepping on a bush and flattening it. Turning round he bumped into a tree, which bent over at an alarming angle.

"Hello," said a tiny voice.

"What was that?!" said the giant, startled. He whirled round looking for the voice and knocked the tree right over. "Where am I?"

"Stand still," yelled the small voice. "You're in our farmyard. I suspect you are all my fault!"

"Pardon?" said the giant. "Did you say I'm all your fault?"

"Yes," yelled the small voice. "Only could you whisper because you are deafening me."

"Of course," apologised the giant and stepping back he trod in the pond and got his socks wet.

"Stand still please, before you demolish the whole farmyard," pleaded the voice.

"Where are you?" asked the giant.

"I'm down here, by the well. Perhaps if you bend down, carefully, you might be able to see me."

And so, carefully, the giant bent down and peered at the well. Standing next to it was a little boy with blond hair and very dirty knees.

"Oh," said the giant. "You're a little boy … aren't you afraid of me? All the little boys in my story books are afraid of giants." "No, I'm not afraid," said the little boy.

The giant got down on his hands and knees to get a closer look. "Gosh, your knees are dirty," he said. "Have you been playing?"

The little boy looked at his knees. "Um, yes, I suppose they are a bit dirty. I lost my magic marble and was crawling around looking for it. This is a farmyard you know, so it gets a bit muddy."

"Oh," breathed the giant. "Have you got a magic marble? I've got one too. Here look," and he fished a marble as big as a doughnut out of his pocket.

"Wow," said the little boy. "That's wonderful. I wish I could find mine." Then a thought crossed his mind. "How old are you?" he asked the giant.

8

"Seventy," replied the giant.

"Oh," said the little boy, clearly disappointed.

"But I think ten giant years are the same as one of your years, so I suppose I'm about seven in your world."

"I'm seven too!" said the little boy, "That's, terrific! You know what, I think my marble magicked you here. I was wishing for someone to play with when the air went wobbly. I was so scared I dropped my marble, which was why I was crawling around in the mud looking for it — and then you appeared. What's your name?" he asked. "Mine's Oliver."

"I'm Bertie," said the giant. "I was wishing for a friend on my marble too," and they looked at each other in awe.

"Wow," they breathed together. "Weird!"

Just then a voice called from inside the farmhouse," Oliver, Oliver!"

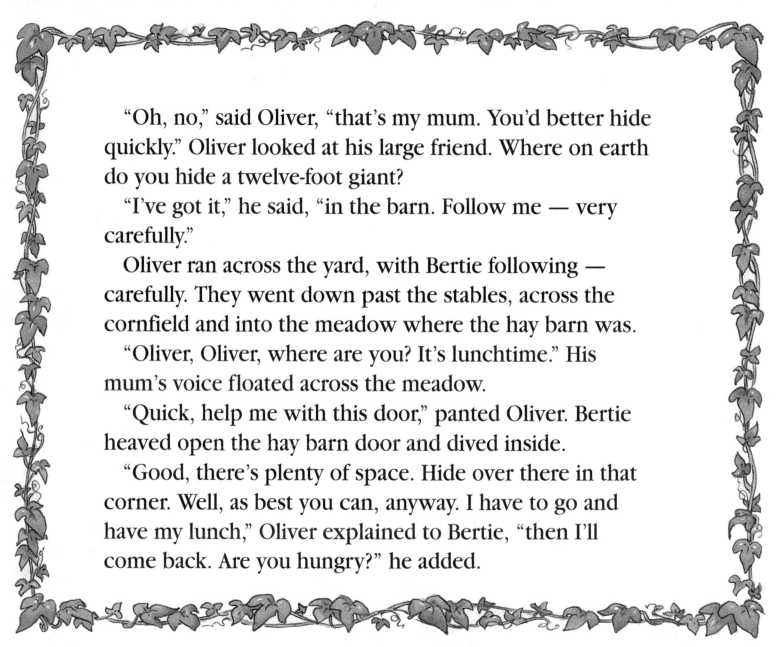

"Oh, no," said Oliver, "that's my mum. You'd better hide quickly." Oliver looked at his large friend. Where on earth do you hide a twelve-foot giant?

"I've got it," he said, "in the barn. Follow me — very carefully."

Oliver ran across the yard, with Bertie following — carefully. They went down past the stables, across the cornfield and into the meadow where the hay barn was.

"Oliver, Oliver, where are you? It's lunchtime." His mum's voice floated across the meadow.

"Quick, help me with this door," panted Oliver. Bertie heaved open the hay barn door and dived inside.

"Good, there's plenty of space. Hide over there in that corner. Well, as best you can, anyway. I have to go and have my lunch," Oliver explained to Bertie, "then I'll come back. Are you hungry?" he added.

Bertie nodded silently, afraid that if he spoke Oliver's mother might hear him. He couldn't stop his tummy rumbling though. It sounded just like thunder.

"I'll try and get you something to eat," Oliver promised and off he went, back to the house for lunch. He gobbled his lunch up as quickly as he could. He could hardly wait to get back to the barn and see his new friend. As soon as he finished eating he rushed back to Bertie.

He had brought Bertie a jam sandwich, which he'd hidden in his pocket. Bertie ate it in one bite. He was too polite to tell Oliver that giants make their sandwiches as big as double beds.

"Now," said Oliver, "we have to find my marble and a way to get you back home. You're too big to stay here and Dad said he had some work to do later in the barn — so we'd better hurry."

Bertie and Oliver crept out of the barn and back to the well. They both got down on their hands and knees and started searching for the marble. They searched and searched, but found nothing.

Eventually Bertie said, "I'm thirsty. Is there any water in your well?" He peered over the edge.

"No," said Oliver, "it's been filled in."

"Wait a minute," yelled the giant, causing the ground to shake and the trees to sway dangerously, "I think I've found it! There's something shining in the earth, about three feet down," and he reached his long arm into the well, fished around a bit and brought out — the marble!

"Hooray! You've found it!" cried Oliver.

"Wow," gasped Bertie. "It's beautiful."

"Right, back to the barn," said Oliver excitedly. "It's time for some magic!"

Back in the barn Oliver and Bertie sat and rubbed their marbles and tried all the magic words they could think of, but the air didn't move, no 'whoomph' sound happened and Bertie stayed firmly in the barn with Oliver.

"Bertie," said Oliver, "would you like to swap marbles — like best friends do? We might even find a way to visit each other." Bertie nodded, smiling enthusiastically, "I'd like you to visit me in the land of the giants," he said.

In the distance Oliver could hear a tractor. "Oh no," he said. "I think my Dad might be coming. We have to think of something, quickly!"

They rubbed the marbles harder and started to invent magic words and all the time the tractor was getting nearer. How would Oliver explain keeping a twelve-foot giant in the barn?

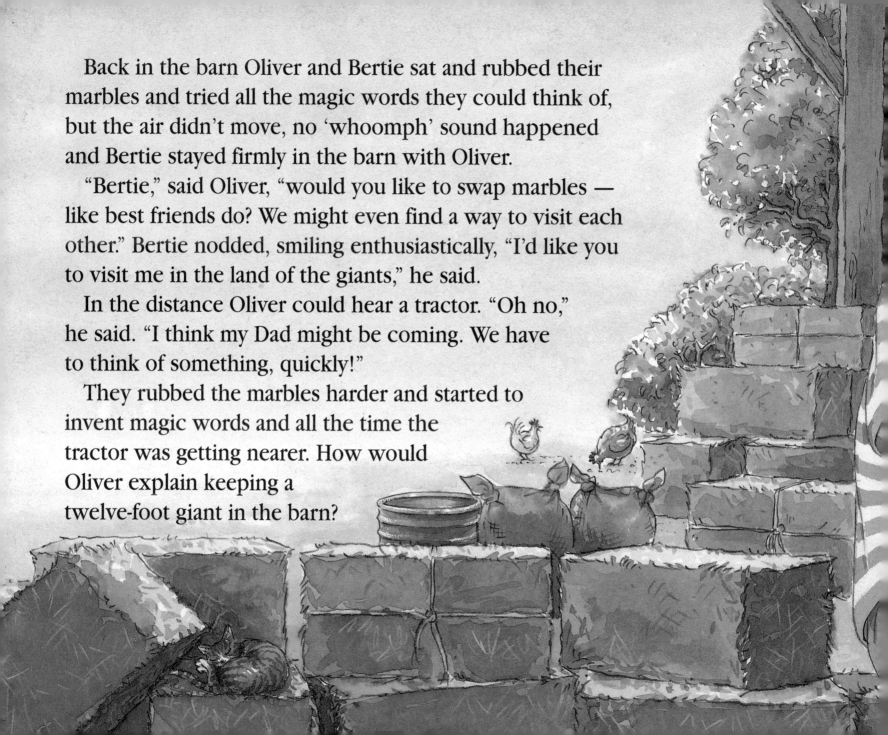

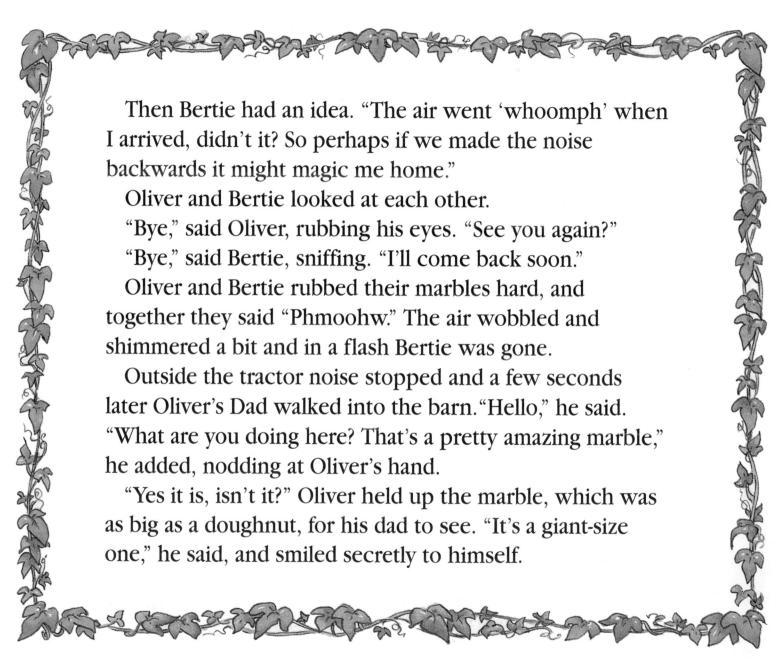

Then Bertie had an idea. "The air went 'whoomph' when I arrived, didn't it? So perhaps if we made the noise backwards it might magic me home."

Oliver and Bertie looked at each other.

"Bye," said Oliver, rubbing his eyes. "See you again?"

"Bye," said Bertie, sniffing. "I'll come back soon."

Oliver and Bertie rubbed their marbles hard, and together they said "Phmoohw." The air wobbled and shimmered a bit and in a flash Bertie was gone.

Outside the tractor noise stopped and a few seconds later Oliver's Dad walked into the barn. "Hello," he said. "What are you doing here? That's a pretty amazing marble," he added, nodding at Oliver's hand.

"Yes it is, isn't it?" Oliver held up the marble, which was as big as a doughnut, for his dad to see. "It's a giant-size one," he said, and smiled secretly to himself.

BIGGER, BIGGEST, BEST

WRITTEN BY DAN ABNETT

Fortyodd was a giant. He was called Fortyodd because he was forty-odd times as tall as a man. His hands were as big as bulldozers and his feet were as big as barges. He was huge. If you spread your arms out wide, it wouldn't be as wide as his smile.

Fortyodd was a gardener. He looked after the Great Forest. He strode through his forest in the way a farmer marches through his cabbage patch, bending over to prune an oak tree here, leaning down to replant a birch tree there.

Fortyodd liked his job. Fortyodd liked the Great Forest. He called it his lawn.

One morning, his friend Fiftytimes came round and knocked on the door of his shed. Fortyodd's shed was nine times as large as an aircraft hangar, so the echo of Fiftytimes' knock rolled round the hills and dales for a week or two.

"Morning, Fiftytimes," rumbled Fortyodd as he came to the door of his shed, a steaming vat of tea in his hand. "The reservoir's just boiling. Do you fancy a vat of tea?"

"Don't mind if I do," replied Fiftytimes.

Fortyodd washed up another vat in his swimming pool-sized sink. He used a small evergreen tree as a brush. "Sugar?" he asked.

"Two barrows, please," replied Fiftytimes, making himself comfortable on the sofa. It wasn't a sofa, actually. It was a small hill that Fortyodd had dragged into the shed and covered with a circus tent, but they called it a sofa.

Fortyodd scooped two wheelbarrows of sugar into Fiftytimes' vat of tea and stirred it with a lamppost.

"So what can I do for you?" Fortyodd asked as they settled down to their vats of tea.

"I thought I had better tell you," said Fiftytimes, "old

Twoscore is planning to enter his prize cabbage in the Harvest Show next week. He's hoping to win the Big Veg prize."

"I didn't know Twoscore had a prize cabbage," said Fortyodd, rather uneasily.

"That's why I thought I'd better tell you," said Fiftytimes. "I was passing his garden just yesterday, and I saw his cabbage patch. It's a handsome crop he's got."

Fortyodd frowned. His brow crinkled so deeply, you could have lost whole flocks of sheep in the wrinkles. You see, every year, his famous pumpkins won the Big Veg rosette at the Harvest Show. There wasn't a giant in the land who grew vegetables that were bigger or better or more beautiful than Fortyodd's pumpkins.

"How are your pumpkins doing this year, anyway?" asked Fiftytimes.

Fortyodd took his friend out into the garden and showed him. There were a dozen splendid pumpkins, each one the size of a hot air balloon.

"Very impressive," said Fiftytimes, "but I have to say, old Twoscore's prize cabbage is bigger than your biggest pumpkin."

Fortyodd was very unhappy. After his friend had gone, he stomped about his garden, grumbling and moaning to himself. The ground shook, and from a mile away it sounded like a serious thunderstorm. Fortyodd tried to do some weeding to take his mind off it, pulling up some chestnut trees, roots and all. But his heart wasn't in it. He went back to his shed and slammed the door behind him.

Fortyodd knew that he had to do something quickly, or Twoscore would win the prize. Fortyodd was very proud of the row of Big Veg rosettes over his fireplace, and couldn't bear the thought that there wouldn't be a new one to pin

up this year. Besides, Big Veg was all he knew. It was his speciality. He hadn't got a particular talent for any of the other prize categories like jam making or tree arranging. Big Veg was his thing. He was a Big Veg giant.

Fortyodd took down the gardening book that his grandfather, old Seventysomething, had compiled. It was chock full of splendid tricks and tips. If nothing else, old Seventysomething had been the tallest gardener of his generation.

Fortyodd laid the book open on his desk. The open book was as wide as the wingspan of a jumbo jet. Fortyodd put on his reading glasses (two telescope lenses from an observatory held in carefully bent scaffolding) and studied the book carefully, slowly turning the rugby pitch-sized pages.

Finally, just as it was getting dark, he found something.

There on page four thousand and one was a recipe for Plant Growth Formula. It seemed his grandfather had got the recipe from a retired witch.

That evening, Fortyodd made up the recipe. It took hours of careful mixing, measuring and stirring. At last, he was sure he had it pretty much right. He poured the formula out of the cement mixer and into a huge pair of furnace bellows. Then, with his lamp in one hand and the bellows in the other, he went out into the dark, to his pumpkin patch nearby. The pumpkins looked huge and golden in the moonlight.

Fortyodd took the bellows and pumped a spray of formula over his prize vegetables. The magic formula twinkled electric green in the darkness. Satisfied with a job well done, Fortyodd admired his handiwork. Already, the pumpkins looked even more huge and golden. Then Fortyodd went off to bed.

Next morning, Fortyodd's alarm (a church clocktower on the bedside table) woke him at eight, and he was surprised to see that it was still dark. He went to the door and tried to open it, but it wouldn't budge. He went to the window, and found he couldn't see anything outside except a wall of bright orange.

Rather worried, Fortyodd took the door off its hinges and found that the doorway was completely blocked by the biggest pumpkin he had ever seen. It was acres across from side to side. Fortyodd squeezed out of the doorway and climbed up onto the top of the enormous vegetable.

High up on top, it was like standing on an orange mountain, and there were several other orange mountains next to it. The huge pumpkins completely surrounded his garden shed, and seemed in danger of crushing it.

The formula had certainly worked.

Fortyodd wasn't really sure what to do next, but he knew that, one way or another, it would involve a lot of pumpkin-eating.

Everyone thereabouts agreed that Fortyodd's pumpkins were the biggest Big Veg they had ever seen. People flocked from miles around to see them. Families of giants had their photographs taken posing in front of the great pumpkin range. Passing dragons looked down at the pumpkins in astonishment. Dwarf mountaineers climbed them and stuck flags in the top.

Twoscore's prize cabbages won the Big Veg rosette at the Harvest Show, of course. Everyone said it was a shame. Fortyodd's pumpkins were the biggest in the world, but even with his friend Fiftytimes' help, he couldn't budge them an inch, let alone take them to the show! Still, he knew one thing — his grandfather would have been proud of him!